SOUTH HOLLAND PUBLIC LIBRARY

3 1350 00246 9981

DISCARD

W9-AYX-924

South Holland Public Library
South Holland, Illinois

Slithery Jake

by Rose-Marie Provencher

illustrated by Abby Carter

HarperCollins Publishers

SOUTH HOLLAND PUBLIC LIBRARY

DISCARD

Slithery Jake
Text copyright © 2004 by Rose-Marie Provencher
Illustrations copyright © 2004 by Abby Carter
Manufactured in China by South China Printing Company Ltd.
All rights reserved.   www.harperchildrens.com

Library of Congress Cataloging-in-Publication Data
Provencher, Rose-Marie.
Slithery Jake / by Rose-Marie Provencher ; illustrated by Abby Carter.
p.   cm.
Summary: A rhyming story about the hysteria that ensues when a
new pet snake is found missing from his cage.
ISBN 0-06-623820-X — ISBN 0-06-623821-8 (lib. bdg.)
[1. Snakes as pets—Fiction.   2. Pets—Fiction.   3. Stories in rhyme.]
I. Carter, Abby, ill.   II. Title.
PZ8.3.B9535 Sl   2004   [E]—dc21   2002023842

Typography by Carla Weise
1 2 3 4 5 6 7 8 9 10
❖
First Edition

3 1350 00246 9981

To Mike, Dan, and Joe,
who understand
—R.-M.P.

To Samantha, Carter, and Doug
—A.C.

Sid came running, skidded to a stop.
"Wait till you see what I just got!
Look, Ma! Look, Pa! I found a snake!
It's my best pet yet, and I call him JAKE."

But Ma's face held a doubtful dread.
"Houses and snakes don't mix," she said.
"Now, Ma," said Pa, "don't fuss and fret.
That slithery creature ain't harmed us—yet."

Next morning at breakfast in a voice full of calm,
Sid announced to them all that his Jake snake was gone.
"He is not in his box, I am sorry to say—

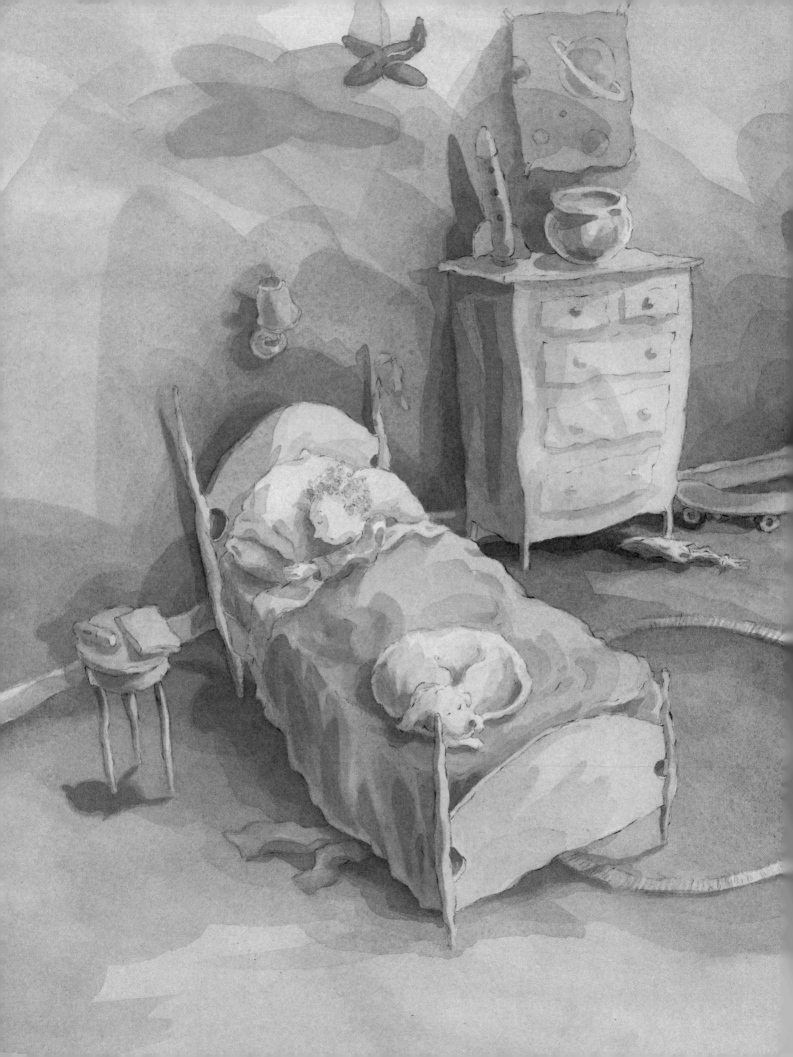

"He has walked in his sleep and meandered away."

Pa choked on his toast.

Ma sputtered her tea.

There were ten thousand spots in the house Jake could be!

Ma started screeching and climbing on chairs.
Aunt Annie went leaping and bouncing up stairs.

She felt safe at the top till she opened a door
And thought she saw Jake curled up on the floor.

She may have moved fast on her speedy ascent,
But she reached twenty G's on her flying descent.

Well, Pa stood there laughing until, by mistake,
He sat on a hot dog and thought it was *Jake*.

And Grandmother fainted while stirring the stew,
For one of the noodles looked like—you know who.

Grandpa grew hungry—he yearned for a munch—
But he feared what he'd find curled up in his lunch.

Dog saw a twitching (a bit of Cat's tail)
And leapt past the light with an ear-piercing wail.

With shuddering shakes, Ma turned down the bed;
Pa tipped up the dish where the hound dog was fed.

Liz set out some cookies;
Sid set out some cake,
But it seemed as if nothing was tempting to Jake.

They looked behind pillows and searched under rugs,
But the only things there were a few surprised bugs.
A puzzlement grew on their worry-filled faces;
They even looked twice in impossible places.

Aunt Annie declared as she ran out the door
She'd never set foot in the house anymore!
"I hear they exterminate snakes, and I bet—"
"No! No!" shouted Sid. "He's my own special pet!"

Pa held up his hand. "Don't worry, Sid.
We'll camp out till we find where the danged thing is hid.
Get the kerosene lamp and the sleeping bags, Liz.
We'll sleep where he *ain't* till we know where he *is*.

"And tomorrow we'll look thirty times everywhere.
Ma, you take the hammock—it's comfortable there."

Ma's only reply was two thunderous roars!
It seems that the snake preferred the outdoors.
For there in the hammock—taking a break,
Stretched out and relaxed—

was
SLITHERY JAKE.